from Mrs. Sitter

for Jake   May 24, 2001

SUPER READER !!

Text copyright © 1986 by Bill Martin Jr. and John Archambault
Illustrations copyright © 1986 by Ted Rand
All rights reserved, including the right to reproduce
this book or portions thereof in any form.
Published by Holt, Rinehart and Winston,
383 Madison Avenue, New York, New York 10017.
Published simultaneously in Canada by Holt, Rinehart
and Winston of Canada, Limited.

Library of Congress Cataloging in Publication Data
Martin, Bill, 1916–
White Dynamite and Curly Kidd.
Summary: Lucky Kidd watches her father ride a mean
bull at the rodeo and thinks about becoming a bull
rider herself.
[1. Rodeos—Fiction. 2. Fathers and daughters—
Fiction] I. Archambault, John. II. Rand, Ted, ill.
III. Title.
PZ7.M356773Wh 1986   [E]   85-27214
ISBN: 0-03-008399-0

First Edition

Printed in Japan
10 9 8 7 6 5 4 3 2 1

ISBN 0-03-008399-0

By Bill Martin Jr.
& John Archambault

Illustrated by Ted Rand

Holt, Rinehart and Winston / New York

It's about time, Dad.
  Yep.
Are ya' scared?
  Nope.
I am.
  Don't need to be.
I just can't help it.
  Guess not.
Why don't ya' get scared, Dad?
  I think.
About what?
  About places.
What kind of places?
  Places I'd like to go.
  Places I'd like to see.
I'd like to go ta' Riverton
to see Grandma.
  She'd like that.

Here comes Dynamite, Dad.
   Yep.
They're puttin' him in the chute.
   Yep.
He sure looks mean.
   He's mean all right.
But a mean bull means extra points.
   Yep.
So you were lucky to get him, huh?
   Yep, luck of the draw.
They say he's the meanest bull
in the whole United States.
   Yep.
But you're the best bull rider
in the whole United States
. . . and Canada, huh?
   Could be.

He sure looks mean, Dad.
   Yep.
Maybe he's just actin' mean.
   Nope, he ain't actin'.
   He's natural mean.
Double-rank mean, huh?
   Yep.
Maybe I'll be a bull rider
when I grow up.
   Could be.
Would you like that, Dad?
Me bein' a bull rider?
   Sure, why not?

I'd want ever'body to know
that Curly Kidd's my dad.
   Me too.
So I'll be Number 13, too
just like you.
   13—2.
   Good number.
And my rodeo name'll be
Curly Kidd's Little Kid.
Do you like that, Dad?
   Nope.
Then I'll just use my plain ol' name,
Lucky Kidd.
   Sounds good to me.

Ya' want a stick of gum, Dad?
   Thanks.
You can have two if ya' want.
   Thanks.
I always chew two, too.
Keeps me calm.
   Me too.
Do you want another stick?
You can have three if ya' want.
   Nope . . . two'll do.

The bull's in, Dad.
Here goes.
    Yep.
Are you all set?
Rope tight?
    Yep.
Good luck, Dad.
Have a safe trip.
    Yep.

Oh, I'm so scared.
I gotta think hard about places . . .
to keep me calm . . .
        Riverton Wyoming . . .
        maybe Casper
        an' Cheyenne
Another place
I wanta go
        . . . someday . . . is

Oh!
He's outa the chute!
Gone plumb dumb wild!
    KAN-sas
    TEX-as
    U-tah
    MAINE

That bull's pitchin'
with all his might . . .
twenty-four tons
a' White Dynamite!

Stick with 'im, Dad!
   AL-*a*-BAM-*a*
   MINN-*e*-SOT-*a*
   IN-*di*-AN-*a*
   AR-*i*-ZO-*na*

Leapin' like a bull frog . . .
    O-*ma*-HA *ne*-BRAS-*ka*
Dustin' up the Big Sky . . .
    KET-*chi*-KAN *a*-LAS-*ka*
Landin' hard . . .
    new MEX-*i*-CO

Four seconds down, Dad!
Four more to go!

Oh! Dad's in the rocker now . . .
floppin' back and forth!
His head's goin' south!
Bull's goin' north . . .
An' I'm goin' ta'
        WEST *vir*-GIN-*ia*
        PLAIN *vir*-GIN-*ia*
        CAL-*gar*-Y *stam*-PEDE!

Oh, that bull's twistin' . . .
twistin' like a corkscrew
straight down the right-a-way.
His middle name's Doomsday!
    U! S! A!

You're winnin', Dad!
You're winnin'!

Rackin'!
Crackin'!
The bull's sky trackin' . . .
tiltin' to the right
in a belly roll . . . .

Say hey Willie May!
Ya' lucked out, Dad
with your left-hand hold!
        ver-MONT!

. . . Oh, my gosh!
There goes my gum!

He's hookin' right!
Now hookin' left!
Only one second left, Dad!
Keep him covered.
Stick to him like glue!

Yah! Hoo!
    KAL-*ama*-ZOO
Tic! Tac! Toe!
    I-*da*-HO

You did it, Dad!

RIV-*er*-TON
an' WAL-*la*-WAL-*la* WASH-*ing*-TON!

Hey, Dad!
You did it!
You won, Dad!
You won!
You prouded me, Dad.
You sure prouded me.
You rode him like glue!

You hear that, Dad?
97 points!
97 out of a hun'erd!
I guess that makes you
the best bull rider
in all the United States!
—*and* Canada!
—*and* Mexico!
    97 ain't perfect.
In my book it is.
You're perfect, Dad!
Total!
All together,
top to bottom,
inside out,
and outside in,
my dad is total perfect!
    That's a lotta words, Lucky.
Hey, Dad!
You're limpin'!
    Am I?

Are ya hurt?
    Don't know.
Don't know?
You oughta know.
It's your foot!
    Can't tell.
How come?
    My head's still ridin' that bull.
Well, my heart's still ridin' too, Dad.
It's takin' an awful poundin'.
    Well, ya' better get used to it, Lucky . . .

. . . if you're gonna be a bull rider.